For you, reader, who can do anything
And for my dad, who taught me I could too —SS

To my family. —VM

This is an Arthur A. Levine book
Published by Levine Querido

LEVINE QUERIDO

www.levinequerido.com · info@levinequerido.com
Levine Querido is distributed by Chronicle Books LLC

Text copyright © 2021 by Sigal Samuel
Illustrations copyright © 2021 by Vali Mintzi

Library of Congress Control Number: 2020937512
ISBN 978-1-64614-037-4
0623/B2269/A8
Printed and bound in China

Published in February 2021
First Printing

Book design by Semadar Megged
The text type set in Brioso Pro Medium

Vali Mintzi painted the artwork for this book with gouache colors in layers. She started out with a rough pencil sketch of the composition, then moved to a transparent, monochrome layer (red for illustrations of daylight and mauve for those of night), after which she added layers of gouache color. For the final layer, Vali inserted details with a thin paintbrush; faces, expressions, patterns of carpets and cloths, stars in the depths of the night.

Osnat and Her Dove

The True Story of the World's
First Female Rabbi

written by **SIGAL SAMUEL**

illustrated by **VALI MINTZI**

LQ

LEVINE QUERIDO

Montclair • Amsterdam • New York

Almost five hundred years ago, when almost everyone believed in miracles, a baby girl was born in the Middle East. Her name was Osnat. Nobody knew it yet, but she would become the first female rabbi in history.

Osnat grew up surrounded by books in the city of Mosul. Her father, Rabbi Samuel Barzani, built a yeshiva, where men studied Torah all day long.

Because Rabbi Barzani often traveled from town to town building more yeshivas, Osnat spent many hours alone with books. She stared and sniffed. She peeked and poked. What secrets were they hiding?

"Show me how to read," she begged her father one day. Rabbi Barzani said, "Girls spend their time on chores. Reading is for boys."

But Osnat replied, "You don't have any boys. If your daughter wants to learn, why not teach her?" And so he did.

Osnat loved the shapes of the Hebrew letters. One looked like a mysterious animal, and another, a creeping vine. She also loved the answers that the Torah's words provided. Each gave rise to seven new questions in her mind.

During one of her father's travels, Osnat watched from her window as a white dove landed in a nearby tree. She brought him some leftover kubbah from her dinner and dropped it into his open beak. This spicy treat became his favorite snack.

Over time, Osnat read to the dove whenever she was lonely. She felt as if he were reading along with her. In this way, they became good friends.

One day Rabbi Barzani returned from a long trip and gazed at his daughter. "You look very grown up," he said. "Soon it will be time for you to get married." Osnat crossed her arms and objected. "If I have a husband, he'll expect me to do chores, and I won't have enough time for Torah study!"

Rabbi Barzani agreed that would be a waste of Osnat's curious mind, so he told all the young men who came to visit that they couldn't marry his daughter unless they promised to excuse her from doing chores. The men were shocked. "No cooking? No cleaning? No thank you!"

But one man, Jacob, was different. He swore that if Osnat married him, she could study Torah all day long. Osnat smiled and asked her father to write up her ketubah, her wedding contract. Then she married Jacob, dancing outdoors as musicians trumpeted on the zurna and drummed on the davul.

Jacob kept his promise and the couple raised a happy family. But eventually Rabbi Barzani passed away. Osnat cried, missing her father, and her dove cried with her.

Jacob became the head of the yeshiva. But he was too busy with his own Torah study to teach the students. They grew restless and rowdy.

Osnat knew something had to be done. She began to teach the students herself. As she spoke the Hebrew words, she felt comforted, as if her father were close by.

For years, Osnat taught Torah. But then Jacob passed away. Osnat was heartbroken. And with her husband gone, there was nobody to take over as head of the yeshiva. No one had ever heard of a woman leading a yeshiva anywhere in the world. Could Osnat do it?

In bed, she tossed and turned.
What would the students think if
she officially became their leader?

One night, Osnat's father came
to her in a dream. He didn't
speak, but—as if to give her a
sign—he smiled at her.

The next morning, the students smiled, too. They already knew what a smart and kind teacher Osnat was. Now she was going to be their leader! What could be better than that?

One day, while Osnat was home preparing her Torah lessons, she heard loud noises through her window: a sharp cry, a soft thump, then screams. She ran outside.

A hunter was standing over her pet dove! The dove's wings were very still. Children were screaming at the hunter, "You shot the bird!"

Osnat didn't say a word.
She took her beloved pet
inside and closed the
door. The hunter and
children waited outside.
They waited. And waited.
And waited.

Finally the silent air filled with rustling. The door opened and the dove came flying out! The crowd looked at Osnat with astonished eyes. Had she healed him?

Rumors of Osnat's power spread across the city. Many came to her for blessings. The sick, the poor, the heartbroken—all believed she had the power to heal them.

At Osnat's yeshiva, the men called her Tanna'it, a title given only to the most respected teachers. They said she knew the deepest secrets of the Torah and that's where her power came from.

Rabbis from near and far began sending her letters. One called her "my mother, my rabbi."

Another letter invited Osnat
to celebrate Rosh Hodesh,
the holiday of the new moon,
with the Jews in the town of
Amadiya. Osnat traveled there
with her dove.

When she arrived, Osnat
was disappointed to see
that the townspeople were
celebrating inside their
synagogue in the weak light
of a few candles. "Come
and dance outside," she
said, "in the light of the
beautiful new moon!"

They celebrated under the open night sky, dancing and singing—until they smelled smoke. It was a good thing they were all outside. The synagogue was on fire! The precious Torah scrolls were still inside.

Osnat acted fast: She whispered the secret Hebrew names of angels, which her father had taught her. At the same moment, her dove flew into the sky. Some of the panicking people, peering through the smoke, thought they saw the bird multiply into many birds. Some thought they saw angels. The white creatures beat the flames with their wings until they put out the fire. Then they disappeared.

When the smoke cleared, the townspeople found that the synagogue was not burned. The Torah scrolls inside were not burned either. The people were so grateful to Osnat that they renamed the synagogue after her.

After a long life of leadership, Rabbi Osnat Barzani died and was buried in Amadiya. People from all over came to visit her grave. They continued to ask for her blessings, believing she had the power to heal them.

Today, her story lives on in the legends of Iraq. They tell of a woman with a curious mind, kind heart, and, according to some, miraculous power—the first female rabbi in history.

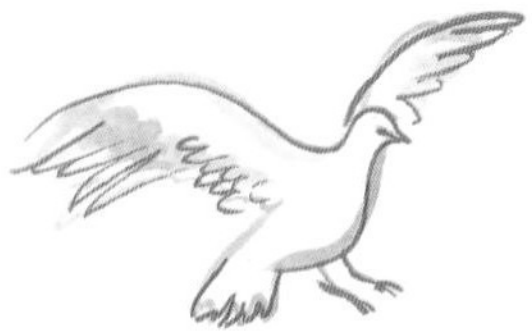